Mark Banana and the NEW, RED CAPE!

by Marcus MacGregor

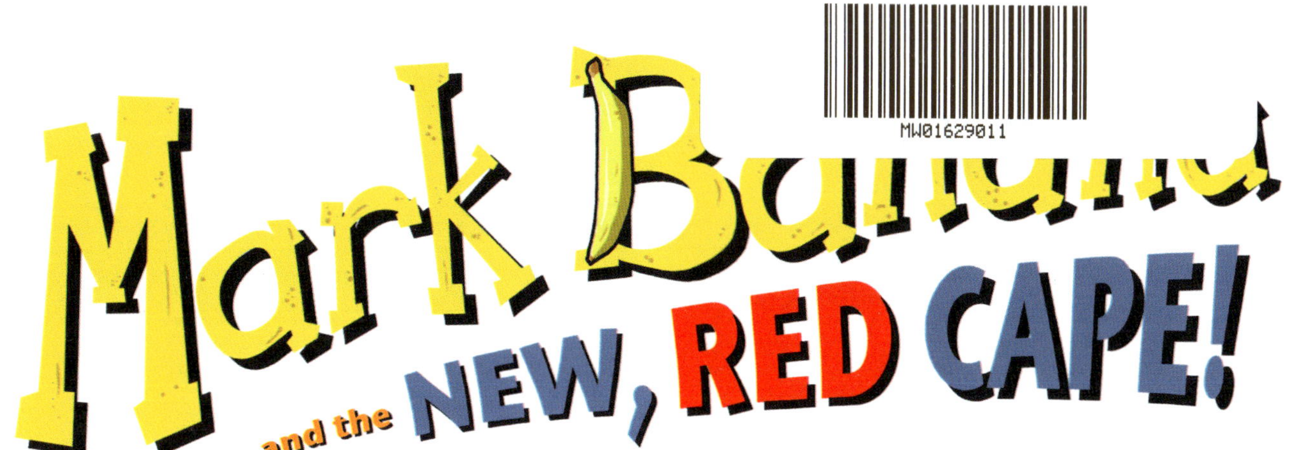

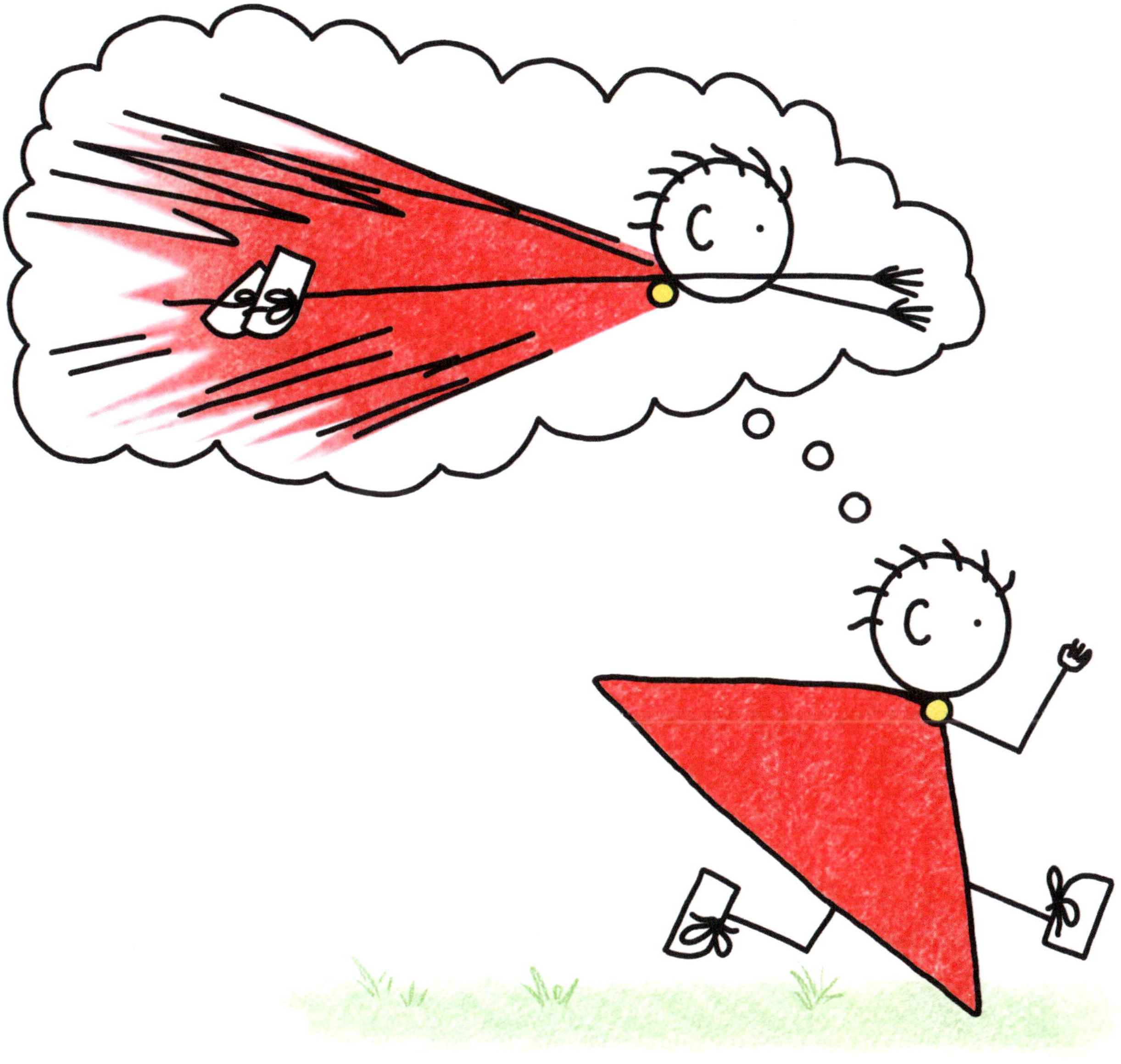

SADDLE SORE Entertainment, LLC

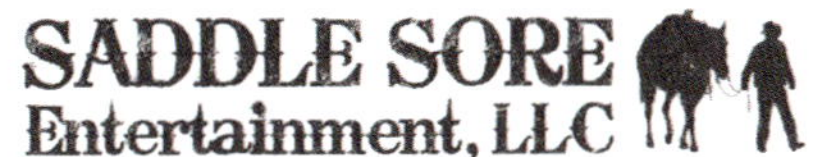

ISBN-13: 978-0615959818
ISBN-10: 0615959814

This book is historical fiction...

For Mom...

This is a story about a boy named Mark.

He liked to ride his bike.

He liked to draw things.

But most of all, he liked to Pretend.

He would pretend he was a prince...

...or a superhero.

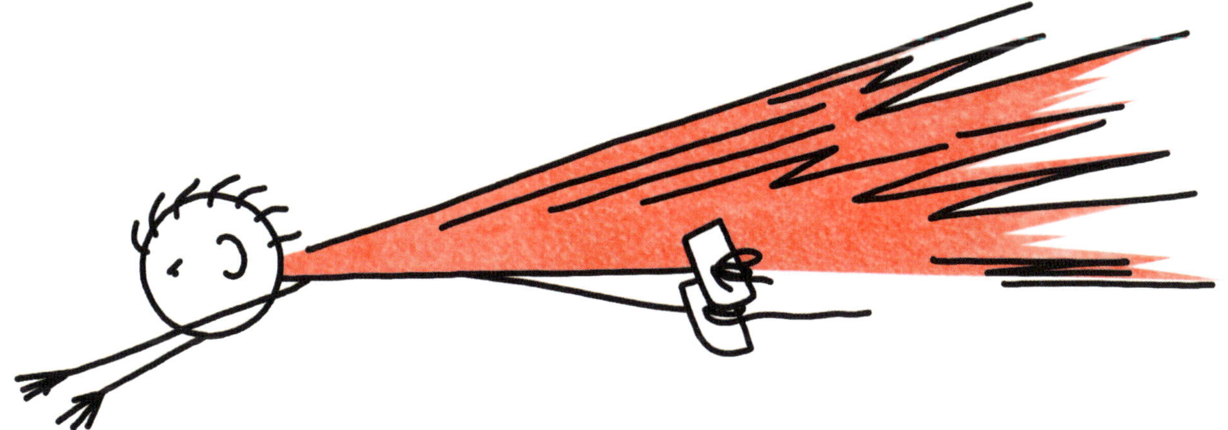

Usually, he needed a cape.

Sometimes he would use a towel...

...but towels were too tight, and they strangled him.

Sometimes he would use a blanket...

...but blankets were too long, and they made him trip.

"You are so silly," his mother would say to him. "That is why I call you my Mark Banana."

One day, Mark said to his mother, "I need a cape so I can pretend I am a prince and a superhero."

"Why don't you use a towel?" asked his mother.

"They strangle me."

"How about a blanket?"

"They make me trip."

"Well then," said his mother, "I guess we will just have to make you a real cape."

Mark and his mother went down into the basement and found a big trunk. Inside were lots of old blankets and curtains.

Mark found a thick red blanket that looked perfect.

"This one," he said.

"Hmm..." said his mother. "It is a little thick... but I think my sewing machine should be able to handle it."

First Mark's mother traced out a pattern...

...then she cut the blanket...

...stitched together the pieces...

...and sewed on a big gold button to fasten it in front.

It seemed to Mark to take forever, but finally his new cape was ready.

His mother draped it over his shoulders, fastened the button in front, and stood back to take a look.

Somehow the cape had not turned out exactly the way Mark had imagined it.

Instead of draping nicely around him to the ground, it stuck out straight and stiff like it was made out of cardboard.

"Ooops," said his mother. "I guess the material was a little too thick."

Mark just stared down at the cape. He didn't know what to say, but he didn't want to hurt his mother's feelings, so he said, "I love it."

But when he got back to his room, he said, “This cape STINKS!” Then he threw it in a corner and said, “I am never going to wear that stupid cape!”

That night he had nightmares.

The next day, Mark ran around outside a little...

...he drew a few pictures...

...and rode his bike for a bit.

But he did not Pretend.

After a few days, however, Mark became bored with running and drawing and bike riding...

...and he decided that he needed to Pretend.

“I’ll just use a towel for a cape,” he said.

But of course the towel was too tight.

“I guess I’ll use a blanket, then,” he decided.

But of course it was too long.

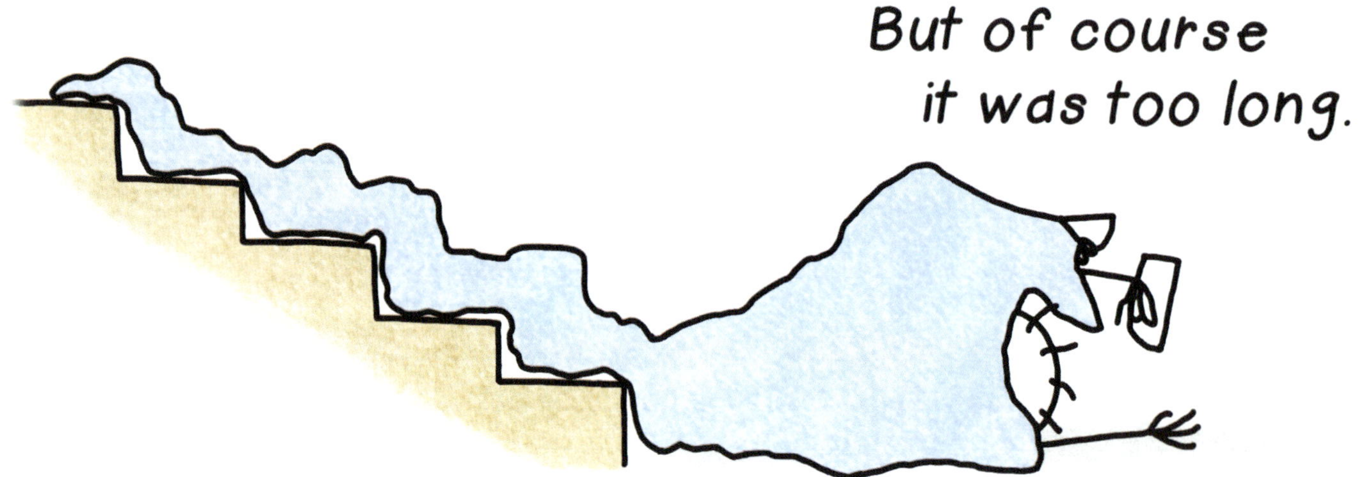

He moped and pouted for a little while.

Finally he said, "I guess I will have to wear that stupid cape, because I am tired of being strangled and falling down. But I still hate it."

Because he was upset about the cape, Pretending was a little hard at first.

But after a while, it became easier.

"I guess maybe it's not as bad as I thought at first," he admitted.

"Oh," said his mother when she saw him. "I see you have on your new cape."

"I love it," he replied. But inside he thought, "I don't love it. But I guess it's O.K."

The next day, Mark drew a few pictures and rode his bike a little, but what he really wanted to do was Pretend again.

His brother Noah was coming inside from playing when he saw Mark wearing his new red cape. Immediately Noah burst out laughing.

"What is so funny?" said Mark.

"You are," replied Noah. "That cape makes you look like a dork!"

Mark was a little embarrassed, so he said, "You are just jealous because you do not have a new red cape. I am no dork, but you are a SUPER DORK!"

As Mark walked off, he said, "Laugh all you want. I am going out to Pretend!"

Mark played by himself for a little while, but soon he decided he needed some friends to play with, so he went down the street to find some other kids.

When he got to Bobby's yard, he saw that all of the other kids were there playing super-heroes. They all had their own capes on.

Bobby spotted Mark coming, and stopped. "Hey, guys," he said. "Check it out." Then they all stopped and watched Mark as he walked over to them. For a minute, nobody said anything.

Then Bobby snickered, "What's that you're wearing?"

"It is my new red cape," Mark said proudly, although inside he was a little hurt that they couldn't tell what it was.

"Oh," said Bobby. "It doesn't really look like a cape. What do you think, Johnny?"

"I think it looks like a tent," said Johnny. Then they all started laughing.

That made Mark really angry. He clenched a fist and yelled, "The next person who says anything about my cape, I am going to mash his face into a pile of DOG POO and cram WORMS up his nose! Now... does anyone have anything more to say?!"

Nobody said anything.

"Good," said Mark. "Now let's play superheroes."

They all played for several hours, but then it started to get chilly. "I'm going inside," said Bobby. "I'm cold."

As it got more and more chilly, one by one the others went home, too.

But Mark wasn't chilly at all. "My new cape is so warm!" he said. "I could stay out and play all night!" Then he played Pretend by himself until his mother called him home for dinner.

"How is your new cape working out?" his mother asked him.

"I love it," he said. But inside he thought, "Well, I don't really love it, but I like it a lot."

That night he wore his cape to bed.

The next day before Mark went to school, his mother said, "Now, my little Banana: your brother will be riding Trent's bus this afternoon to play at his house, and I have a dentist's appointment. I should be home before you get back from school, but in case there is a delay, I am giving you this key so you can get inside the house. Do you think you can hold on to this key and not lose it at school?"

"Of course I can," said Mark.

"You are sure?" asked his mother.

"I am sure," he replied.

"One hundred percent sure?"

"One hundred percent sure."

"Alright then," said his mother. "Are you wearing your cape to school today?"

"I think so," said Mark. "But I will probably take it off and put it in my cubby so Jason Malloy does not tease me."

"That sounds like a good idea," said his mother. "Have a good day, and don't forget your lunch."

Mark went out to the bus stop, and soon the bus came to take him to school.

He wore his cape on the bus, but when he got to school he took it off and hid it in his cubby before Jason Malloy saw him.

All day, Mark dreamed about Pretending. At recess, he played kickball because that was what all the others were doing. But he couldn't wait to get home and play Pretend with his cape.

It seemed like forever, but finally the bell rang and the day was over. Mark grabbed his cape, snuck past Jason, and took a seat on the bus.

When he got home, Mark ran to his house to grab a quick snack.

His mother was not home yet from her dentist's appointment, so Mark reached into his pocket for the key she had given him. But the key was gone.

"I am in trouble now," he said. "Mom is going to kill me when she gets home."

Mark sat on the steps and waited.

"I am sure Mom will be here soon," he said. But five minutes went by, and she had not come home.

"She will be here any minute now," he said. But five more minutes went by, and still she had not come.

"It is really chilly," said Mark. "It is a good thing I have my new cape on. It is so warm, I can barely feel the cold."

Finally, after what seemed like forever, Mark's mother pulled in the driveway.

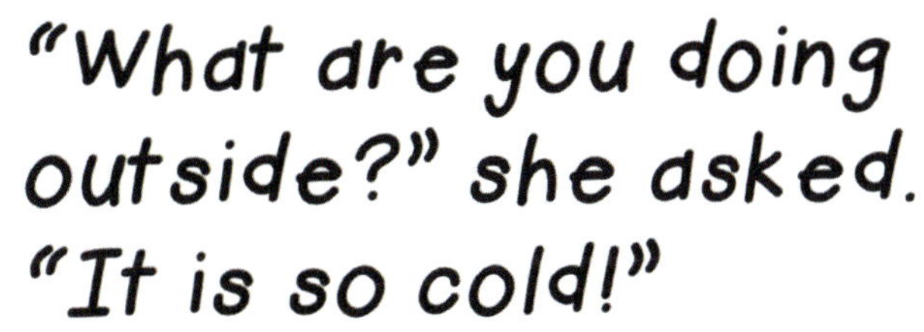

"I lost the key," said Mark. "But I wasn't cold at all. My new cape felt just like a warm hug. Are you going to kill me?"

"No, my little Banana," his mother smiled down at him. "I am not going to kill you. I am just glad you were not too cold."

From then on, Mark wore his cape wherever he went (but he still hid it in his cubby at school so he wouldn't get teased).

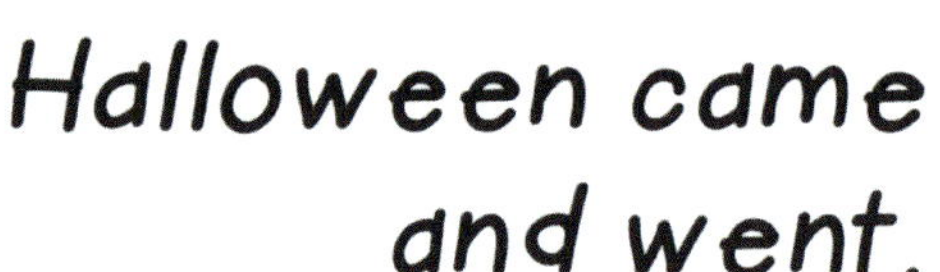

Halloween came and went.

So did Christmas.

And finally Spring came.

One day when most of the snow had melted, Mark said to his mother, "I am going outside to play Pretend."

That was when his mother noticed there was a hole in the back of the cape.

"Mark," she said, "there is a hole in the back of your cape. You wear it so much that you have worn a hole right through it. Maybe it is time for me to make you a new cape."

But Mark said, "NO! I do not want a new cape. I want you to fix this one."

"But I could make you a brand new one that drapes nicely to the ground instead of sticking out funny," said his mother.

"I don't care if it sticks out funny," said Mark. "I want only this cape."

"Well," said his mother, "I suppose I could put a patch over it. I just thought you were never too happy with this cape."

"That's ridiculous," said Mark. He unfastened the button and held up the cape for his mother to fix. "I love this cape," he told her.

And this time, he really meant it.

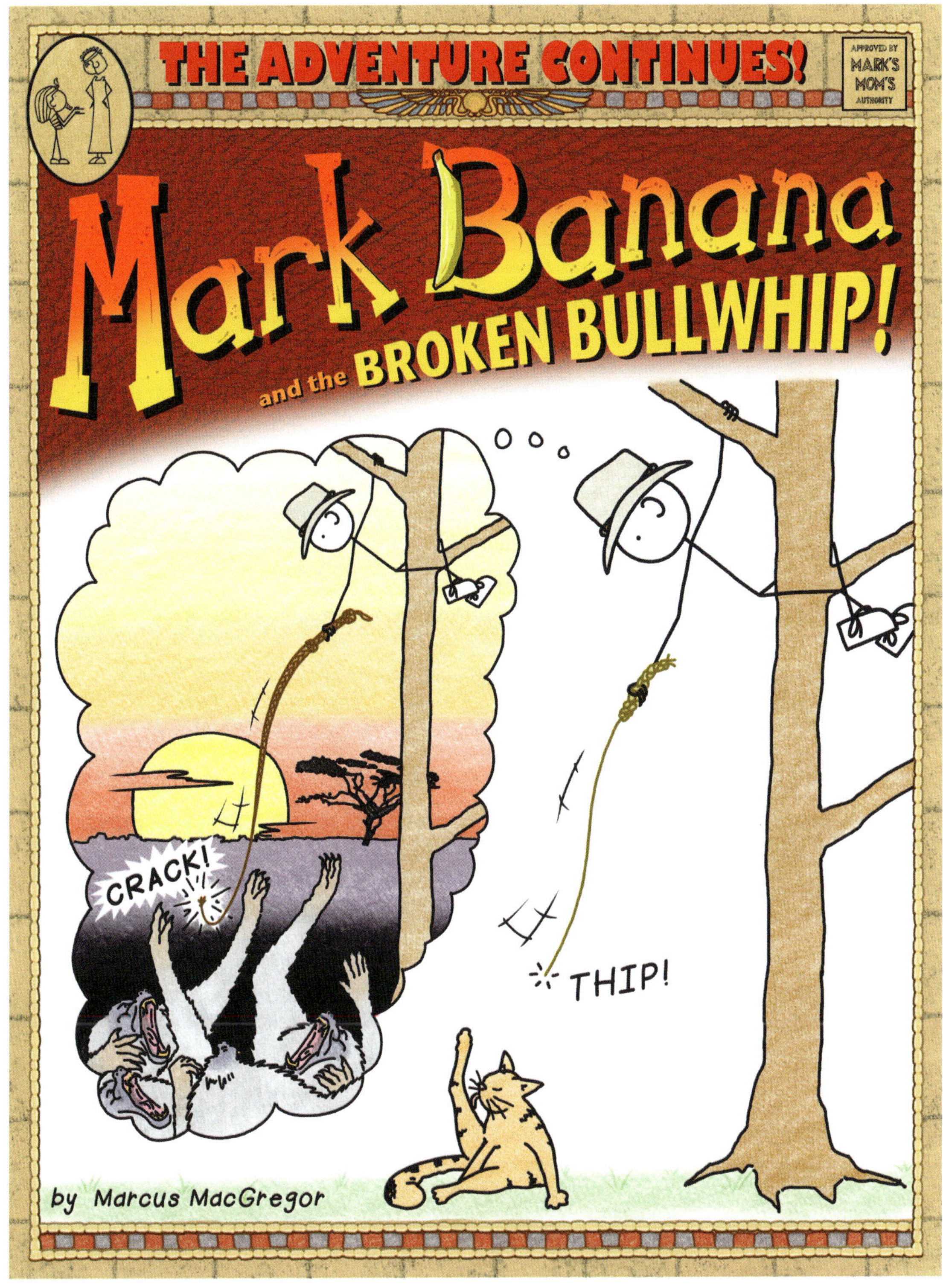
THE ADVENTURE CONTINUES!
APPROVED BY MARK'S MOM'S AUTHORITY
Mark Banana
and the BROKEN BULLWHIP!
CRACK!
THIP!
by Marcus MacGregor

29351866R00029

Made in the USA
Charleston, SC
11 May 2014